Taking Care of Tucker

Taking Care of Tucker

Pat Lowery Collins
pictures by Maxie Chambliss

G. P. Putnam's Sons   New York

Text copyright © 1989 by Pat Lowery Collins.
Illustrations copyright © 1989 by Maxie Chambliss.
All rights reserved. This book, or parts thereof,
may not be reproduced in any form without permission
in writing from the publishers. Published simultaneously in Canada.
Printed in Hong Kong by South China Printing Co.

Library of Congress Cataloging-in-Publication Data
Collins, Pat Lowery.   Taking care of Tucker.
Summary: Millie knows her three-year-old cousin
will love the way she takes care of him when his
parents go away—even though he does kick and
spit and scream at her.
[1. Cousins—Fiction] I. Chambliss, Maxie, ill.   II. Title.
PZ7.C69675Tak   1988   [E]   88-4057
ISBN 0-399-21586-7

First impression

To Colleen

PLC

My name is Millie. That's short for Millicent. I am an only child. This means that I am the only child in my family.

My Aunt Violet and Uncle Joe have an only child too. His name is Tucker. When I saw him last, all he could do was sleep and eat. But Tucker is three, now. I'll bet he walks and talks like a person.

"He is a person," my mother tells me.

Well, anyway, Tucker is going to stay with us while Aunt Violet and Uncle Joe take a trip. I can pretend he's my baby brother. I know he'll love the way I take care of him.

"Tucker is here," my mother says.

He has a little suitcase, a blanket, and an ugly, squishy bunny. I have a better bunny than that for him.

He starts to cry as soon as Aunt Violet and Uncle Joe leave. He sits on top of his suitcase and his blanket, and sobs. His bunny gets all wet and sloppy.

"Don't worry, Mother. I'll take care of Tucker," I say.

She goes upstairs to make his bed.

I know that if I put my arms around him and sing to him, he'll feel fine again. I do this and

he kicks me in the stomach!

Then he takes his ugly bunny and goes into
the closet. He doesn't stop crying. He falls
asleep in the closet.

"Doesn't he look sweet when he's sleeping?"
my mother says.

He doesn't look like he would kick me in the
stomach.

"I'll carry him up to bed for a nap," she says.
I carry the soggy bunny.

His bed is in my room. I decide that when he wakes up I'll read to him and we can play games.

I lie down on my bed and wait.
Tucker sleeps a long time.

At last, when I see him moving around, I put my face against his pillow and say, "Hi!"

He opens his eyes wide. He really does look cute.

He spits at me!

"He's just feeling homesick," my mother says. "He misses his mother and father."

Tucker sits in his bed and stares straight ahead. He won't get up.

I tell him a story about Aunt Violet and Uncle Joe and the places they will visit.

He starts to scream!

"You'll have to be patient," my mother says. "This is all new to him."
This is new to me, too.
But I can take care of Tucker. He'll find out what fun we can have together!

At dinner, Tucker sits in my old highchair next to me.

"Here we go!" I say, giving him a spoonful of spinach. I make the spoon fly like a plane.

Tucker just looks at me.

"He can feed himself," my mother says.

She gives him his own plate with little bits of everything.

"Look! He can! He really can!" I say.

"And isn't he a neat little fellow?" says my mother.

She has made his favorite pudding for dessert. He likes it. He claps his hands and says, "Goody!"

He dumps it on my head!

Now Tucker is laughing—hard.
I really want to hit him—hard.
But Mother says, "He was just having fun, Millie. You mustn't mind."
I wash my hair and pretend not to be mad.

After dinner, we play Wild Animals on the floor. My father is the Papa Tiger. Tucker is the Baby Tiger. I decide to be the Big Bad Bear.

I growl softly so that I won't frighten Tucker. I run slowly around the room, letting him catch me. He catches me.

He bites me!

This time I cry. He has sharp teeth.

"Tucker thinks he's a real tiger," says my father. "I'm sure he didn't mean to hurt you."

I'm not sure.

"I think he hates me," I say.

"Of course he doesn't hate you," says my mother.

"I hate her!" says Tucker.

"Help me give Tucker a bath," my mother says.

We fill the tub and undress him. Tucker runs away and hides under the bed. We pull him out and put him in the tub.

"Look at him splash like a seal!" says my mother.

Then comes the first wave over the edge.

Mother slips on the floor. I trip over Mother. We are both soaking wet. But Tucker slides happily from side to side. He is so soapy and slippery, we can't lift him out.

"Help us!" my mother calls to my father.
"Hey, big guy," Father says, reaching for
Tucker, "Upsy Daisy!"
But instead of Tucker coming up, my father
goes down.

"Do something, Millie!" yells my mother.
So I pull the plug.
My mother throws a towel at my father. I can't quite hear what he is saying under it.
"I'm cold," says Tucker.
I wonder if seals ever shiver like that.

"Bedtime for Tucker," says my mother.
She puts him in bed with his old blanket,
and I give him the beautiful bunny I got last
Easter. That will make him love me!

He throws it across the room!

Then Tucker rolls on top of his old bunny
and blanket, and falls asleep.

When I go to bed, Tucker is making loud buzzing noises in his sleep.

"Be quiet!" I say, but he still buzzes. He keeps me awake with his noises.

I pick up my beautiful bunny from the floor
and stuff it under him, and I put the squishy
bunny in the bottom of the dirty clothes
hamper.

There! Tucker isn't making
a sound. Now I
can go to sleep!

Early in the morning while it is still dark,
something wakes me. Tucker is crying like a
baby. He is looking at the beautiful bunny and
crying softly and very sadly.

"I can't get any sleep around here!" I say.

I turn over and put the pillow over my head.

A long time later, I take the pillow away, and he is still crying.

I listen awhile. Then I get up and dig around in the clothes hamper for the ugly bunny.

"Here," I say. "You can have the old thing back if you want it so badly."

Tucker stops crying.

"It's about time!" I say and go back to bed.

The light is just beginning to come through my window when I feel a little warm body against my back and two worn bunny ears scratching my neck.

"It's me," says Tucker.

"No buzzing," I answer.

I knew all along he'd love the way I take care of him.